This Walker book
belongs to:

- - - - - - - - - - -

For
Jonathan and his
big sister, Ellie,
with love –S.L.-J.
For
Sally Lloyd-Jones
–S.H.

WALKER BOOKS
AND SUBSIDIARIES
LONDON • BOSTON • SYDNEY • AUCKLAND

First published in Great Britain 2008 by Walker Books Ltd
87 Vauxhall Walk, London SE11 5HJ

This edition published 2009

10 9 8 7 6 5 4 3 2 1

Text © 2007 by Sally Lloyd-Jones
Illustrations © by 2007 Sue Heap

The right of Sally Lloyd-Jones and Sue Heap to be identified as author and illustrator respectively of this work
has been asserted by them in accordance with the Copyright, Design and Patent Act of 1988.

Published by arrangement with Random House Children's Books, a division of Random House, Inc.,
New York, U.S.A.

This book has been typeset in Stempel Garamond

Printed in China

British Library Cataloguing in Publication Data: a catalogue record for this book
is available from the British Library

ISBN 978-1-4063-2333-7

www.walker.co.uk

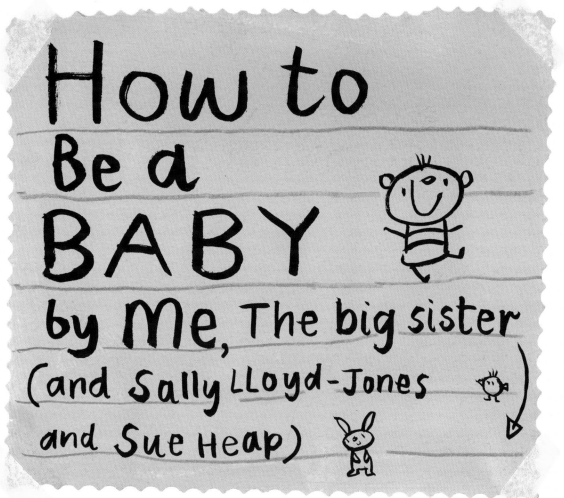

How to Be a BABY

by Me, The big sister

(and Sally Lloyd-Jones and Sue Heap)

When you're a baby, you are in a cot and not in school.

When you're a baby,
you just wear your pyjamas ALL THE TIME
and not real clothes.

Your mummy and daddy
have to dress you
because you don't know how.
(But I do.)

When you're a baby,
it's not good because
you don't have any hair.
(I have long hair like a princess.)

When you're a baby,
you don't read books.
You eat them.

You don't understand TV.

People talk to you,
but you don't know what it means.

You talk, but no one knows what you're saying
because you just make it all up.

You sing songs,
but you don't know the words.
Or the tune.

(I know the words and the tune AND THE DANCE.)

When you're a baby,
you don't carry a backpack.
You go in one.

And you can only sit.
You can't stand,
or walk,
or go
ANYWHERE.

People have to carry you
EVERYWHERE.

(This is you being carried
EVERYWHERE.)

HERE'S WHAT ELSE YOU CAN'T DO:

- ☆ Run or hop or skip or swim
- • Ride a bike without stabilizers
- ♥ Ride a bike with stabilizers
- ☆ Climb on the monkey bars all by yourself
- • Bounce on the trampoline (it's SO EASY)
- ☆ Use scissors
- ♥ Be a princess or a fairy or a mermaid
- ! Actually anything really fun

When you're a baby,
your mummy and daddy have to feed you
because you don't know how.

You don't have any teeth AT ALL.

You can't eat normal food.
You can only eat yucky baby food.

HERE'S WHAT ELSE YOU CAN'T EAT:
- Pizza
- Chocolate
- Chocolate ice cream
- Chocolate cake
- Anything good

When you're a baby, you are scared of your potty.

HERE'S WHAT
ELSE YOU ARE
SCARED OF:

* The Sea
! Grandma's Shiny
  Black Shoes

Father Christmas
* Big Ted
* Actually lots of
not-scary things
at all

When you're a baby,
you're called Pudding or Pumpkin or Sweetie or Dumpling,
and people say,

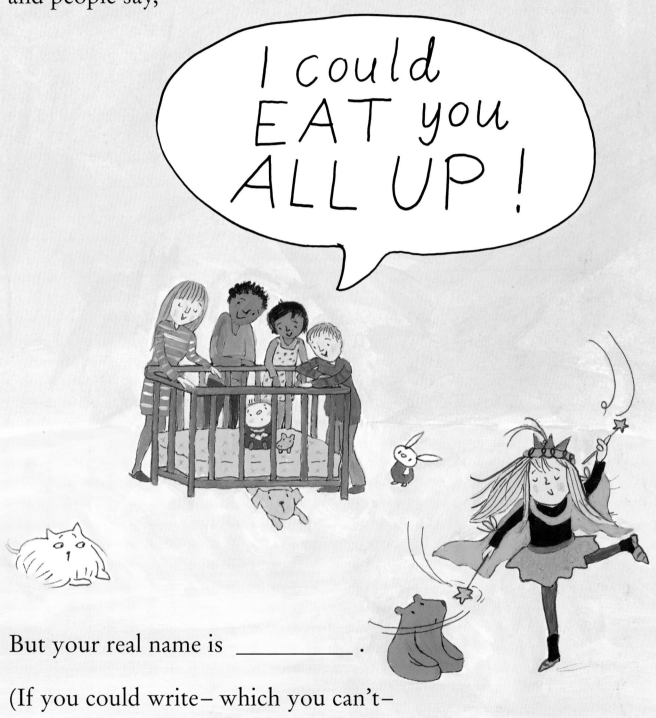

I could EAT you ALL UP !

But your real name is _____ .

(If you could write– which you can't–
you would put your name in that space.)

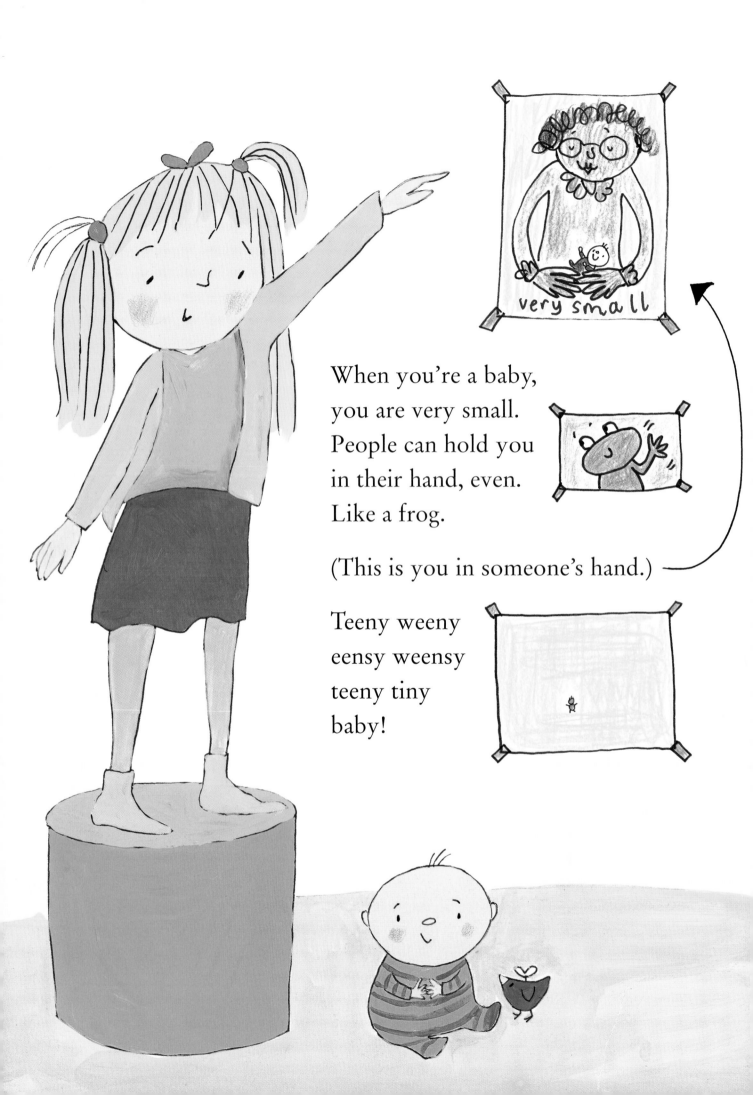

When you're a baby,
you are very small.
People can hold you
in their hand, even.
Like a frog.

(This is you in someone's hand.)

Teeny weeny
eensy weensy
teeny tiny
baby!

When you're a baby,
you are a different shape.

You are round.

But then you get bigger
and your legs stretch out
and your tummy gets long
so you don't look so fat
like a big balloon
with a belly button
sticking out.

round

getting
Longer

When you're a baby,
you don't know how old you are,
or where you live,
or even if you're a boy or a girl.

HERE'S WHAT ELSE
YOU DON'T KNOW:

Two times two equals
four and there are
only 28 days in February

The opposite of up is down,
the opposite of big is little,
the opposite of you can do
a handstand is you can't
do a handstand

✓ Any secrets
♥ Any jokes
✳ How to make
a snowman

! Anything

I am a girl

MY BOOK of Anything

MY JOKES by me

I am 6

I live at this HOUSE

BIG elephant

UP

down

← little insect

When you're a baby,
baths are not nice.
They are dangerous.
Because you are too slippery
so someone has to watch you ALL THE TIME.

(This is me staying in the bath as long as I want, all by myself.)

When you're a baby, it's not good
because the wind can blow you over.
When you're a baby, people eat your ice cream for you
because ice cream isn't appropriate for babies.

And you're not allowed to TOUCH ANYTHING.

And a special plug goes in your mouth.
It's called a dummy and it's to stop your scream coming out.

When you're a baby,
you don't sit on a chair.
You are tied to it.

Or you fall off and bump your head
and scream and have to go to bed.

And when you go in the car, you have to sit in a
car seat with a handle on it.
You don't even face the right way.

Facing
THE WRONG WAY

me
facing the right way

(I prefer to sit in a seat like a normal person.)

When you're a baby,
you have boring toys
like rattles and bricks.

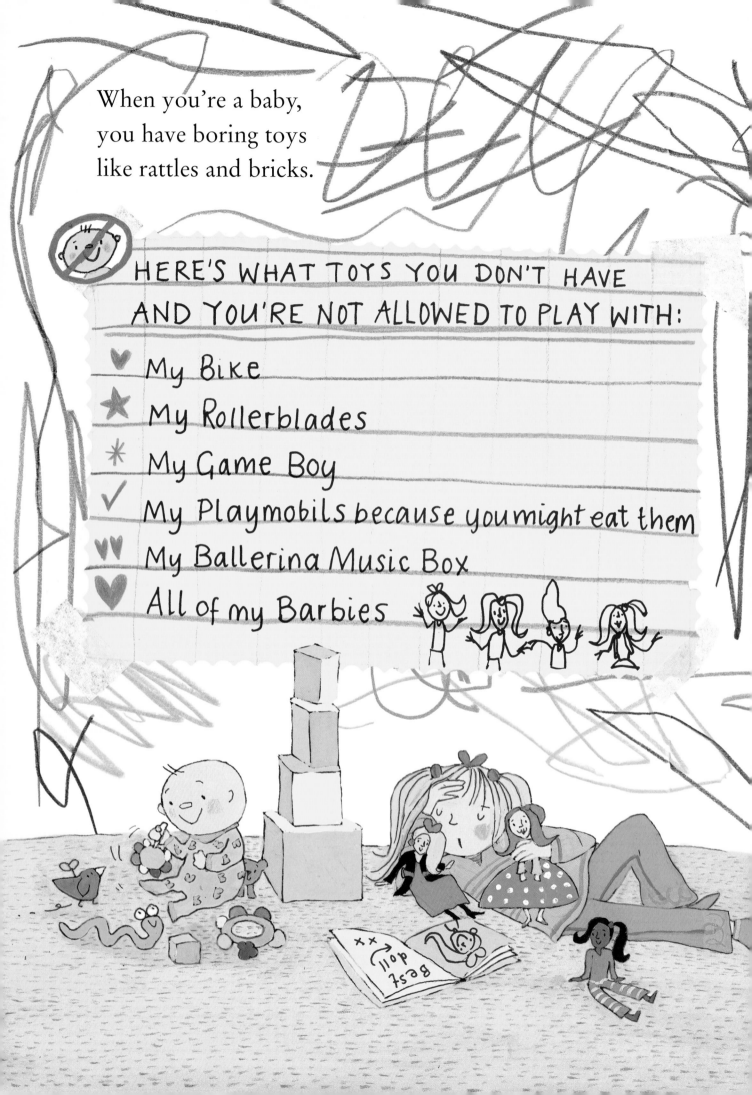

HERE'S WHAT TOYS YOU DON'T HAVE
AND YOU'RE NOT ALLOWED TO PLAY WITH:

- My Bike
- My Rollerblades
- My Game Boy
- My Playmobils because you might eat them
- My Ballerina Music Box
- All of my Barbies

When you're a baby,
you don't have good manners AT ALL.

You pull other people's glasses off,
and grab their noses,
and spit your food on them.

HERE'S WHAT ELSE YOU DO THAT'S ILLEGAL:

- ★ Open other people's presents
- ! Knock other people's castles over
- ! Tear pages out of other people's favourite books
- !! And scribble in them
- ✗ Draw on walls
- !!! Poo on the carpet
- ✗ Other naughty things like that

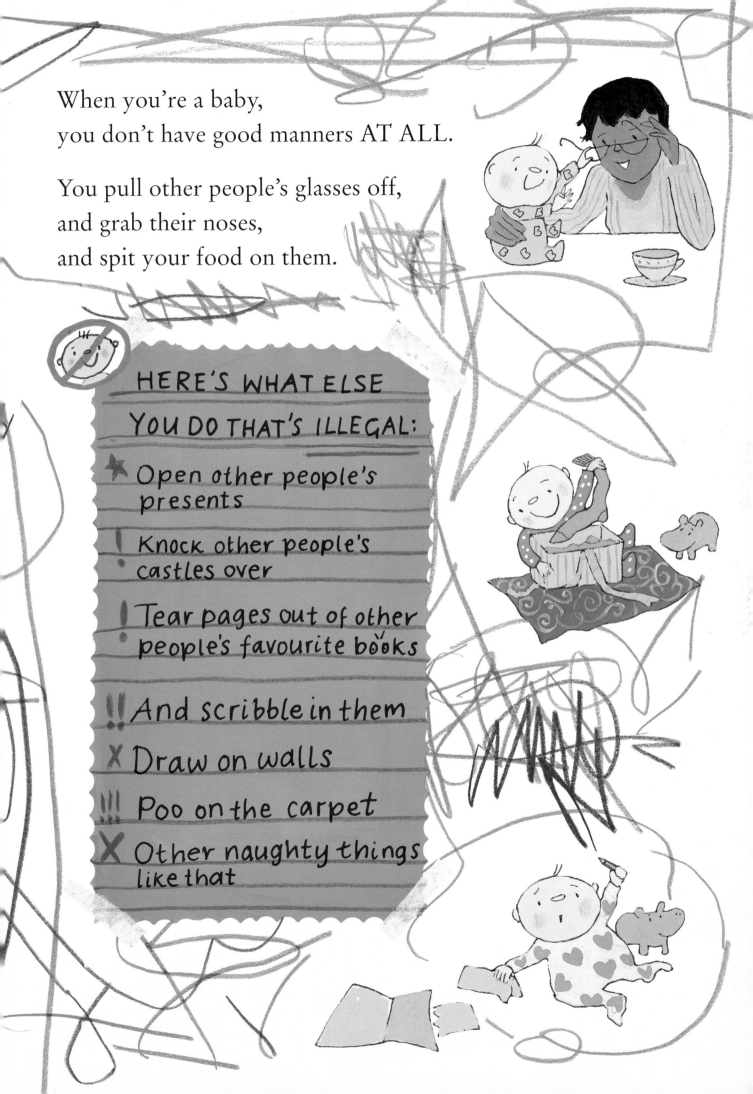

Cats don't like you,
because you pull their tail
and stroke their fur the wrong way.

Sometimes,
if you're VERY naughty,
you are put in prison.

(This is you IN PRISON.)

When you're a baby,
you don't have any real friends.
(I have lots.)

When you're a baby,
you have to have the light on ALL NIGHT
or you get scared.

And you're not allowed to have ANY pillows on your bed.

In the middle of the night,
you wake everyone up
because you cry REALLY LOUDLY
and give me a headache.

And that's when I come in and
whisper to you and kiss you
and tell you, "Don't worry, Baby Dumpling,
it's just a scary dream," and then you feel better.

When you're a baby,
people hug you and kiss you
ALL THE TIME!

(Babies are good at hugging but they can't kiss because
they don't know how their mouths work yet.)

HERE'S WHAT ELSE
BABIES ARE GOOD
AT:
★ Burping
! Peeing
!! Pooing
∧ Crying and screaming
zzz Sleeping
★ Making a mess

It's SOMETIMES nice being a baby
because people don't say,
"Stop being a BABY!"
Because you ARE a baby
and you can't help it,
so it's not your fault.

And people smile at you because you're so small.

And sometimes you are funny
and you make me laugh.

When you get big,
you won't be a baby any more.

But your mummy will still carry you if you're tired.
And your daddy will still sing songs
to you if you can't sleep.

And I will still let you hold my hand when you're afraid.
(Because you will still be a little bit little.)

HERE'S WHAT
ELSE I'LL LET
YOU DO:

Follow me ✓

Copy me ✓

Play with my ✓
friends (sometimes)

Sit in my fort ✓
and have secrets
together

Learn everything
from me so you can
be as clever and ✓
good at everything
as me (almost)

And ONE DAY
you'll be as tall as me!

And then I'll say,
"Remember when you were little? Remember?
How you used to never be able to do ANYTHING,
remember?"

And we'll laugh
and point at pictures of you in the olden days
when you were a baby.

Also by Sally Lloyd-Jones and Sue Heap

ISBN 978-1-4063-2343-6

Other books by Sue Heap

ISBN 978-1-4063-1334-5

ISBN 978-1-4063-1485-4

ISBN 978-1-84428-554-9

Available from all good bookstores

www.walker.co.uk